Steal a Swordmaiden's Heart

STEAL A SWORDMAIDEN'S HEART

COURT OF MIDSUMMER MAYHEM

PREQUEL

TARA GRAYCE

Chapter One

Theseus, king of the Court of Knowledge, stood in his tower study and contemplated whether death or marriage was the better option.

He clasped his hands behind his back, gazing out of one of the windows set into the tower's round walls. This particular window looked over the Great Library, the magical library that was the heart and soul of this Court. Currently, the sunlight winked off the glass dome and all the glass skylights, but sometimes in the evenings, Theseus could see through the dome to the upper shelves of books, lit with the golden glow of the faerie lights.

There was a reason he preferred to work tucked away in this tower, leaving the official study on the main floor for formal occasions or meeting with visitors from outside of his court.

All the knowledge of the Fae Realm, and it was his to protect.

For more centuries than anyone in this realm cared to

count, his ancestors had protected the Great Library. He could not be the first to fail.

If only his circumstances weren't so dire, his choices so desperate.

A knock came on the door. Theseus didn't turn around. "Enter."

The hinges creaked, followed by two sets of expected and recognizable footsteps.

Philostrate, Theseus's steward, cleared his throat. "Your Majesty, I have brought Head Librarian Marco, as you requested."

"Thank you." Theseus could not bring himself to turn around. "What is the latest report from the Court of Revels?"

"My sources confirm that tension between King Oberon and Queen Titania is rising. At this point, they can't even stand to be in the same room without fighting." Philostrate's voice remained steady and formal. "A resolution does not appear to be coming anytime soon."

Theseus suppressed a sigh. Bad enough that the barrier between the Fae Realm and the Realm of Monsters had been wearing increasingly thin lately all over the realm. But with the magic of Midsummer thinning the barrier even more, this Midsummer Night was shaping up to be deadly. To make their situation even worse, King Oberon and Queen Titania's marital fighting would also create thin spots in the barrier. Possibly even tear a full hole.

On Midsummer Night, monsters would pour from their realm into the Fae Realm, wreaking havoc on anything in their way.

And the Court of Knowledge didn't have enough trained warriors to withstand the onslaught.

Thus Theseus's dilemma. If he did nothing, he would most likely die on Midsummer Night along with the rest of his Court as they struggled to protect the Great Library from destruction.

Or, he would have to forge a bargain with another Court, one with warriors aplenty who could protect both their Court and his. Yet the only bargain strong enough —and safe enough—would be for him to be bound in marriage to a relative of a Court ruler. Or, better yet, the ruler herself.

That left Theseus with precious few options. The king of the Court of Stone had a daughter that Theseus could attempt to steal. As did the king of the Court of Sand. But both of those courts had so many monster attacks of their own that they had no warriors to spare to aid another Court.

That left Queen Hippolyta of the Court of Swordmaidens. She was unmarried, near to Theseus's age, and her island court of warrior women was strong and relatively untouched by the monster attacks. She would have plenty of warriors to spare to defend the Court of Knowledge.

The only problem was that Theseus could not merely steal Queen Hippolyta the way he would a bride from another court. Stealing a spouse was a time-honored tradition among most of the Courts, but the Court of Swordmaidens had their own, unique traditions that governed them.

Theseus drew his shoulders straight, still staring

down at the Great Library. "Marco. What did you find about the marriage bindings practiced by the Court of Swordmaidens?"

"Sadly, not much." Head Librarian Marco's tenor held the regret of a researcher bemoaning the knowledge of a long-lost civilization. "The Court of Swordmaidens has always been secretive when it comes to marrying into their Court. They don't allow men to stay on their island, and when I've sent female librarians to their island to research their ways, the librarians always end up taking their side and never provide me with the information I'm looking for. Any time I manage to document anything, that information always mysteriously goes missing from the Library. I don't even know how they pull that off."

Theseus's fingers hurt from gripping them so tightly behind his back. That wasn't the answer he had been hoping for, though it was the one he had expected. The swordmaidens guarded their secrecy fiercely. They so rarely left their island that Theseus didn't even know what Queen Hippolyta looked like.

He turned to face Philostrate and Marco. Philostrate was a thin fae male with earnest blue eyes and black hair flecked with gray. Marco wore his black librarian coat with gold embroidery that marked him as the head librarian of the entire Court of Knowledge. His white beard hung all the way to his knees.

These two men were Theseus's closest, most trusted advisors. He needed their support of this plan, no matter how desperate it was.

Theseus leaned against the windowsill, facing them. "Is that all the information you could find?"

"Yes, that's all the officially documented information." Head Librarian Marco gestured, his fingers catching in a few strands of his beard. "But I've been around for a while. I've heard a few things. I know that a swordmaiden's hand can never be stolen, only won. When you present yourself to attempt to win a swordmaiden's hand, you'll be put through tests to prove your worthiness. If you pass the trials, you will win the hand of your chosen swordmaiden. If you fail, you will be tossed from their island, never allowed to return. If you survive."

Trials. Most likely of strength, endurance, and warrior skills. Things a swordmaiden would appreciate in a mate.

Theseus had trained with the best warriors of his Court, as well as a few warriors from other Courts from whom he had managed to bargain training sessions in exchange for particularly sensitive information they had been seeking from the Library. Surely he would have enough experience and skills to at least hold his own long enough to pass their tests.

Though, the tests they would inflict on him to win the hand of their queen would be brutal.

"What of their famed labyrinth?" Theseus tried to sound casual. "I am guessing that will be one of the trials?"

Marco gave a nod. "Most likely. There are stories that the labyrinth connects to other parts of the fae world, and thus it isn't as secretive as some of the other aspects of the Court of Swordmaidens. From my research, the key to navigating the labyrinth is to go forward, always down, and never left or right. But more than that or what the other trials might be, I cannot say."

It was about what Theseus had expected, though it would have been nice to have more information to better prepare for what he would be facing.

"Are you sure about this, Your Majesty?" Philostrate regarded him with a bland expression, not giving away his own thoughts on the matter besides the ones revealed in his question. "You can't afford to be killed. The Court will need you to lead us on Midsummer Night."

Philostrate had a point. They only had two moons until Midsummer Night. If Theseus died—without an heir as he was—the Court of Knowledge would be plunged into leaderless chaos right before the most dangerous Midsummer they had experienced in a long time.

Theseus gritted his teeth, staring Philostrate down. "If you have a better option, then name it."

Philostrate snapped his mouth shut and looked away. Even Head Librarian Marco shifted and wouldn't meet Theseus's gaze, and Marco was rarely uncomfortable about anything.

But as the silence stretched long and painful, neither of them offered any suggestion at all, much less a better one.

That was what Theseus thought. He had no choice. He either won the hand of Queen Hippolyta and bargained for her help on Midsummer Night or he and his Court would face a desperate last stand to stave off the coming hordes of monsters.

"As none of us can think of a better option, there is

no sense in putting this off." Theseus faced his two advisors, wiping any dread from his expression or voice. "I don't know how long it will take or how long I will be gone. Philostrate, I will do my best to send messages back through the Anywhere Door as often as I can."

"Yes, Your Majesty." Philostrate bowed, tense grooves cutting across his face. "I will update you on any developments as I can, assuming the swordmaidens allow messages to reach you."

"Head Librarian Marco…" Theseus trailed off, not sure what to say. If Theseus died without an heir, the nobles would squabble over who had the most claim to the throne. It would be up to Head Librarian Marco to sort out the mess.

"I understand, Your Majesty." Marco gave a sharp nod before he disentangled his fingers from his beard. "Just see to it that you return safely. It would save all of us a great deal of trouble."

That it would.

"Trust me. I have no intention of dying." Theseus rested his hand on the sword he had belted to his waist.

Neither Marco nor Philostrate pointed out that having no intention of dying did very little to prevent someone from getting killed if he found himself outmatched. But the looks they both gave him said they were thinking it.

Besides the two advisors in this room, Theseus had no one to tell farewell before he left. No one besides the people in this room would even care if he died, besides the inconvenience and chaos it would cause in their lives. A few of the courtiers might even rejoice at his death, since it would give them a chance at claiming the throne for themselves.

The throne was a lonely place to sit, and he couldn't even admit that to anyone. That was a weakness the other Courts and his own nobles would exploit.

And now, if he managed to win Queen Hippolyta's hand, he would be lonely even with his own wife. He could never trust her. She would always place the good of her own Court above his, even if she could be convinced to help.

Then again, she would never trust him either since he would also place the good of the Court of Knowledge over her Court. It was, after all, the reason he was seeking to marry her. All he wanted was a bargain that would save his Court.

Mutual distrust. That was the best he could hope for in this marriage. If he had in his most foolish dreams harbored the hope that someday when he married he would no longer face the isolation of the crown alone, then that dream would have to die.

Theseus glanced over his shoulder, drawing in one more glimpse of the glittering Library dome and the precious books it housed within.

He could handle this. The trials. The future loneliness. The burden of distrusting his own wife. Whatever it took, as long as the Great Library was protected.

Theseus pushed away from the window and strode across the room, nodding to Philostrate and Marco as he passed.

They fell into step behind him, following him as he strolled down the curving stairs of the tower. The stairs ended in a hallway filled with the private rooms reserved for the royal family.

Only one lonely room was occupied.

He traversed the hall, reaching the center entrance of the castle. A large set of double doors took him to the Hall of Anywhere Doors. These Doors connected to places all over the Fae Realm, providing all of the Courts access to the knowledge contained in the Great Library.

Theseus faced the nearest Anywhere Door and rested his hand on the latch. Perhaps he should turn around. Maybe Marco and Philostrate expected him to give a speech or one more set of instructions or something.

But he had said all that needed saying.

Now was the time for action.

Theseus straightened his shoulders, drew in a deep breath, and mentally asked the Door to take him to the Court of Swordmaidens.

When he yanked open the Door, it showed a sunny courtyard surrounded by ivy-draped white columns. Beyond the columns, the spires of a sand-colored palace rose toward the sky.

Without a backward glance, Theseus stepped through the Door and closed it behind him. As soon as the Door closed, two swords flashed, one pointing at his neck, the other at his heart.

Theseus raised his hands, not even daring to turn his head to either side to get a glimpse of the swordmaidens that he could just see out of the corners of his eyes.

"What is your business here?" one of the sword-maidens asked, her sword never wavering from Theseus's neck. "You must know that males are forbidden on this island."

This was it. No going back now.

"I am King Theseus of the Court of Knowledge, and I have come to win the hand of Hippolyta, queen of this Court."

Chapter Two

Theseus held still as one swordmaiden kept the sword pressed to his neck while the other divested him of his sword and his belt, then patted him down, searching for any other weapons tucked away. She didn't find any as he had only taken his sword, assuming that this thorough search would occur.

Once she finished her search, the swordmaiden hurried away, leaving Theseus still menaced at sword point. He resisted the urge to shift or make any gesture that could be construed as discomfort or weakness. From this point onward, he would have to be a warrior, not a librarian king.

That resolution became harder and harder to keep as the time dragged on. What was taking Hippolyta so long to see him? Was she purposely keeping him waiting as a first test?

Probably. He should assume that everything from this point forward was a test of some kind.

Finally, the swordmaiden returned, followed by two

more female warriors. A lot of unnecessary security, considering Theseus was just one unarmed man.

The swordmaidens marched Theseus from the outdoor pavilion containing the Anywhere Door, along a broad avenue with lush gardens on either side, and into the cool interior of the stone palace.

After crossing the entry hall, Theseus was led into a grand throne room. Each side of the room was lined with rows of fully armed and armored swordmaidens, their faces stern and eyes hard. Behind them stood more women, wearing plain white dresses. These must be the servants and other women who lived on the swordmaidens' island.

At the far end of the room, Queen Hippolyta sat regally on a golden throne, her black hair wound in braids and decorated with diamonds. She stared down her nose at him, her dark eyes calculating.

Theseus stood straighter, refusing to be bowed beneath the weight of her glare. He knew what she would see. A fae king with short black hair and wearing a blue coat cut in nearly the same style as the coat worn by the librarians serving at the Great Library. He was not intimidating like many of the kings of other Courts, though he was not as pathetically paunchy either.

Queen Hippolyta lifted her chin, the twist of her mouth disdainful. "What is your business here, Theseus of the Court of Knowledge?"

Theseus refused to flinch under the ice in her voice. "As I told your swordmaidens, I am here to win your hand, Queen Hippolyta."

If anything, Queen Hippolyta's gaze darkened, her

posture stiffening. "Why do you seek the hand of the queen of the Court of Swordmaidens?"

There was something odd about the way that was phrased, but he didn't have the luxury to dwell on it now. Instead, he tried to appear every inch a king, matching her regal glare for regal glare. "As you must know, an especially deadly Midsummer Night is quickly approaching our region of the Fae Realm. The Court of Knowledge does not consist of trained warriors, and we will be overwhelmed if we do not have aid from a warrior Court. Thus I come to you, Queen Hippolyta, to win your hand and bargain with you for swordmaidens to protect the Great Library and the precious knowledge it contains."

If she felt any sympathy for the plight of the Great Library, her face and voice didn't soften. "You have told us what you wish from the Court of Swordmaidens. But what benefit will you provide to my Court? Why should I even entertain your request and not throw you out here and now?"

Theseus studied Queen Hippolyta for a long moment. What could the Court of Knowledge give to this Court?

This had been his hesitation in going to another Court. He had nothing to bargain with. Thus he needed a marriage, not a bargain. He drew a deep breath. All he could do was bluff it out. "I am the king of the Court of Knowledge. I can provide you with unlimited access to the Great Library."

"We already have that, or nearly." Queen Hippolyta waved her hand breezily. "It is the foundational tradition of your Court that you may not deny knowledge to one who comes seeking it."

She had called his bluff. Theseus held her gaze and remained silent. He truly had nothing he could tell her.

"If you are here, then you must have done your research. Or tried to do so." Queen Hippolyta's mouth gave that twist again, this time something almost like a glint of humor in her dark eyes. "You must have realized the lengths we will go to guard our secrets even from the Great Library. Perhaps you could offer to help with that effort, should you win the hand of the queen of sword-maidens."

A spear of ice stabbed his stomach. He opened his mouth, then snapped it shut. Was this all that Queen Hippolyta wanted from him? The one thing he couldn't give. He shook his head firmly. "You know I can't offer that. As king of the Court of Knowledge, I am sworn to conserve knowledge when I find it, not destroy it or hide it."

It was the wrong answer. Of course it was. Theseus struggled not to slump. Had he already failed? Would Queen Hippolyta throw him out immediately? It was her right to deny him even a chance to win her hand, if he was deemed so unacceptable.

But as desperate as he was, he could not break his honor nor ignore a foundational tradition of his Court.

After flicking her gaze to the side, almost as if searching for someone else's approval, Queen Hippolyta tipped her head toward him. "Very well, King Theseus. Your request has been granted. You will endure three trials as you attempt to prove your worthiness for the hand of the queen of this Court. My swordmaidens, please throw him in the dungeon to await his first trial."

The dungeon? Theseus didn't resist as the four swordmaidens shoved him backwards, all but dragging him bodily from the throne room as if he was a criminal instead of a king.

Perhaps dungeon was metaphorical. After all, the dungeon could merely refer to a strong tower. Maybe he would be brought to a nice, guarded tower room. He was the king of another Court. He was due some consideration, right?

✹

APPARENTLY WHEN QUEEN HIPPOLYTA said *Throw him in the dungeon*, she had meant the actual dungeon. Not the nice, guarded-but-opulent suite on an upper floor as Theseus had been expecting, given his rank.

No, he had been dragged to the literal dungeon, complete with faerie steel shackles clamped around his wrists and ankles. He could move no more than three feet from the wall, and the shackles on his wrists held his arms above his head when he sat on the floor. The floor, roof, and three sides were the same sandy stone as the rest of the swordmaidens' palace while the last side was a wall of bars and a barred door that was just out of reach due to the shackles.

It was, admittedly, rather nice as dungeons went. It was situated beneath the sprawling, mostly open-air palace with a small, barred window set high in the wall just above his head, pouring in sunlight and salt-tinted ocean breezes.

He had just enough reach with the chains that he could grip the window ledge and pull himself up to peer out. As the palace had been built at the top of a cliff, he had a gorgeous view of sweeping cliffsides and rolling ocean waves, turquoise near the shore before deepening to cerulean, then richest indigo at the horizon. It was a kingly view, even if the rest of his accommodations weren't.

Theseus leaned against the wall at his back as he sat on the floor, letting his arms dangle from the chains.

He had failed the first test. They had wanted what he could not agree to give.

Had they known that? Was that question purposefully designed to make him fail? Yet if that were the case, then why give him a chance to win her hand at all?

No matter. He would simply have to do better on the next trial, when it came his way.

Perhaps he was already experiencing it? Was being thrown in the dungeon another test? Maybe they were testing his patience or ability to think rationally in unexpected situations. Maybe even humility, if they thought he would complain.

No, he would have to be strategic about this time in the dungeon. He would figure out training he could do while confined and chained to keep his strength up. He would do his best to listen and learn and get the measure of his captors. He would have plenty of uninterrupted time to plan his next moves carefully.

Far more carefully than he had when concocting this desperate plot in the first place.

Out of his sight, footsteps scuffed on the stairs down to the dungeon. Theseus stayed where he was. Not that he could go anywhere, but he made sure he kept his muscles relaxed, his expression neutral, to appear nonchalant about his imprisonment.

A woman dressed in a plain white robe with a wide, leather belt came into view, carrying a tray of food. She wore her thick wavy blonde hair in a simple braid down her back, and she kept her eyes down.

Yet her arms were well-muscled, and her stride held a sure confidence that even her attempts to appear humble couldn't hide. Here in the Court of Swordmaidens, even the servant women were well-trained and warrior-like. Theseus shouldn't let his guard down, even around her.

She balanced the tray on one hand while she unhooked a set of keys and unlocked the barred door with the other.

If he had been in another situation, Theseus might have started plotting ways to get those keys away from her and escape.

But escape wasn't his goal here.

He pushed to his feet as she stepped into the room, the chains rattling.

"Your supper." She thrust the tray at him and finally lifted her gaze to his. Her eyes shone a sharp, light blue that bit into him.

Theseus took the tray, giving her a smile. "Thank you."

He held the tray for a moment, considering his

options. If he sat down, he wouldn't be able to reach the tray if he set it in his lap.

That left eating while standing. He would have to hold the tray in one hand and eat with the other. It would make cutting the piece of mystery meat smothered under a blue sauce a little difficult, but he would manage.

The servant girl continued to stand there, just out of reach of his chains. Her gaze remained sharp and assessing.

Theseus picked up the spoon. Might was well start with the bowl of chopped fruit first before he tackled the meat. As he dug out his first bite, he glanced over the tray at her. "Are you going to watch me while I eat?"

"I am under orders to claim the tray as soon as you finish." The servant crossed her arms, her gaze steady. "And I'm to check that you don't try to palm the knife."

The butter knife was so dull that he didn't think it would do anything against the meat, much less work as a weapon.

"I am right where I intend to be. There won't be any escape attempts." Theseus chewed a bite of fruit, studying her. This might be a test, but that didn't mean he couldn't plot his own schemes. This servant could turn into an asset, if he could get her talking. He gave her what he hoped was a guileless smile. "What's your name? If we're going to be personal enough that you watch me eat, we might as well share names."

Did her mouth twitch at that? Perhaps he was getting somewhere with her.

"You can call me Ariadne, the handmaid to Queen Hippolyta." The servant woman studied Theseus with a frank gaze that seemed far too unflinching for a servant. Then again, this was the Court of Swordmaidens. Her air of confidence might not be so odd.

"It is a pleasure to meet you, Ariadne. Please give my compliments to the cook and to your queen for providing this fine meal." Theseus smiled between bites.

Ariadne raised an eyebrow at him. Just a single eyebrow in a way Theseus had always envied. "Does that charm work on the women of the Court of Knowledge? Because it won't earn you the queen's respect here."

Theseus let the far-too-smarmy smile drop from his face. He had been laying it on a tad thick. "No, it doesn't. My apologies for trying."

He eyed the tray. He'd polished off the fruit. The bread would be manageable with one hand, but after that, he would have only the meat left.

Instead of stabbing the meat with the fork and gnawing on it, he held out the tray to Ariadne. "Would you mind cutting my meat into bite-sized pieces? It would be easier for me to eat with one hand."

That eyebrow shot back up again. Perhaps he had surprised her, with the request that she cut up his food like he was a child. Would she be impressed that he was willing to humble himself to this indignity? Or would she find him demanding?

Whatever she thought, she picked up the knife and fork and sawed at the meat while Theseus held the tray. She had to work at it, confirming his suspicion that the knife was less than sharp.

Theseus tried to think of something else to ask. Charm hadn't worked. Perhaps direct questions would be better. "What can I expect now? Do you know what my first trial will be?"

She shook her head, set down the fork, and stepped back. "Did you really think I would answer that?"

"Not really." Theseus shrugged and reclaimed the fork. "But silence while you watch me eat is awkward. If you have a better topic of conversation, then please tell me."

He inspected the meat. It looked like it might have been some kind of giant bird. Perhaps a roc. They came through the thin spots in the barrier with the Realm of Monsters quite often in this area. A few were even known to roost on some of the rocky, outlying islands.

Would he have to face a roc as one of his trials? Rocs were large and intimidating, but it would be a straightforward monster fight. He could handle those.

Ariadne's mouth quirked, as if he had finally gotten through to her. "I've heard much about the Great Library, but I've never had the chance to walk through the Anywhere Door to visit. What is it like? Is it as grand as all the stories claim?"

The Library. Now there was a topic he wouldn't mind talking about.

Between bites of the meat and bread, Theseus described the Great Library. Its sprawling wings and rooms filled with books from floor to ceiling. Its ancient, slightly grouchy personality as it guarded the books in its possession. The bookwyrms that scurried around the shelves, protecting the books and eating any pests that dared invade the Library.

Ariadne's light blue eyes remained intent as she

listened, asking questions occasionally. By the time she gathered the tray and left, Theseus had some hope that he had made progress in gaining her trust.

Step one in surviving these trials and returning to his Court with the Swordmaiden Queen as his wife.

Chapter Three

Theseus stood in front of a dark hole in the side of a cliff. At his back, Queen Hippolyta loomed in full battle armor, complete with a chainmail tunic and leather bracers. Swordmaidens spread out in an arc on either side and behind her.

Queen Hippolyta's expression remained cold, hard, as she stared Theseus down. "This is your first trial, King Theseus. Inside the labyrinth in the depths of our island lurks a monster. Find it, kill it, and bring its head back to me."

As expected, one of the trials would involve the famed labyrinth. At least Marco had managed to glean some information on it. Go forward, always down, and never left or right. That sounded easy enough. He would have to hope he would stumble across the monster if he followed Marco's instructions.

A swordmaiden stepped forward and held out Theseus's sword.

"And if I fail?" Theseus claimed the sword and buckled the belt around his waist.

"You die." Queen Hippolyta's hard face didn't soften. Her dark eyes didn't warm. If she hoped that he would win her hand, she didn't show it. "If the monster doesn't get you, the labyrinth will. I hope you designated someone as your heir before you left your Court."

A shiver traced down Theseus's back, though he refused to let her words get to him. He would survive. There was no other option.

Instead, he gave her a grin. "Any hints that you would care to share, Your Majesty?"

Her glare managed to turn even colder. "No."

Theseus might have been making progress with the handmaid Ariadne when she brought him his meals, but Queen Hippolyta was a different story. From the time he'd been thrown into the dungeon three days ago, he hadn't seen her again until she had him hauled out and marched to this hole.

He had expected that Queen Hippolyta might be hostile to the idea of marrying him, but facing that hostility was something else entirely. He needed her to protect his Court, not plot to stab him in the back the first chance she got. The last thing he wanted to do was end up in a marriage as unhappy and unpleasant as King Oberon and Queen Titania's.

Should he give up? Call off this attempt to win her hand?

Yet did he dare return to his Court without this warrior woman at his side, knowing the battle that was to come?

"Do you have any last words, King Theseus?" Queen Hippolyta drew her sword, as if prepared to force him to enter the labyrinth.

He was the king over the greatest library found in any realm, yet he couldn't think of anything sufficiently grand to say right then. Besides, these weren't going to be his last words. He wasn't going to die down there.

Instead of stating something melodramatic, he shrugged and strode toward the entrance to the labyrinth as casually as he could manage. "If my steward Philostrate shows up with a stack of paperwork while I'm gone, tell him I'll deal with it when I get back."

Really? That was what he was going to go with? Instructions about paperwork. Theseus suppressed a sigh and stepped into the coolness of the labyrinth. Could he sound any more like a boring king from a scholarly court? Probably not someone Queen Hippolyta would find interesting. She most likely hoped more than ever that this labyrinth or its monster would dispatch him.

The tunnel continued downward for several yards before it ended in a round room, lit from the entrance behind and above him. Three passageways branched from the room.

This was it. The beginning of the labyrinth.

Even as he stood there, the walls in front of him shifted with the grinding of stone and haze of dust. By the time the dust cleared, five passages now faced him instead of three.

Now that would make this complicated. Was the center passage the same one that had been in the center before? Or had the tunnels completely rearranged? Even if he scratched arrows on the wall or floor, the labyrinth might shift whatever markings he left.

A scuffing sound came from the passage on the far left.

Theseus whirled, drawing his sword as he went. Would it be so easy that the monster would just walk right up to him?

A figure in white stepped from the tunnel, her hands raised and her golden hair vibrant even in the low light. As she stepped farther into the light, he could see that she wore a sword buckled at her waist.

"Ariadne? What are you doing here?" Theseus sheathed his sword.

"I've come to help." Ariadne lowered her hands, resting one hand on the hilt of her sword and the other on her hip next to a pouch hanging from her belt. "You'll never survive without help."

"Succumbing to my charms after all?" Theseus smirked, gesturing at himself.

"No. I'm doing this for the Library." She gave him that raised eyebrow smirk right back. "If you don't want my help, I'll leave. Enjoy wandering the unending labyrinth until you die."

"If you don't mind braving a monster and this labyrinth, you're welcome to come." Theseus waved to the passageways. Even as they stood there, the passageways shifted again. Now seven tunnels faced them. "Do you have any wisdom to share about navigating this place?"

Would what she told him match what Marco had found? If it didn't, would that mean that Ariadne was lying to him to mislead him? Or that Marco's research had been flawed?

It was hard to imagine that Head Librarian Marco would present Theseus with unreliable facts. He was meticulous when it came to research.

"As you might have surmised, marking the walls or floor won't work. The best way is to go forward, always down, and never left or right." Ariadne reached into the pouch at her side and pulled out a ball of what looked like yarn. "But it also takes this. Yarn spun from the golden fleece of the sheep found in the highest, most rugged peaks of the Court of Stone. The magic of this yarn will keep the passages we enter from shifting, and we'll be able to follow it back out when we are done."

What was he to make of that? Was the addition of the yarn necessary? Or was it a trick?

So far, Ariadne hadn't poisoned him while he ate. And she had been a pleasant enough companion when she talked with him while he ate his meals.

He didn't dare trust her. But that didn't mean he had to actively distrust her either. He could just go along warily until she proved herself one way or the other.

"Getting back out sounds good." Theseus studied the nine tunnels now facing them. He pointed toward the passageway in the center. "Let's go."

Ariadne tied the end of the yarn to a sconce holding a torch.

Theseus claimed the torch and led the way toward the tunnel. Ariadne kept pace, unrolling the ball of yarn while she went.

As they stepped into the tunnel, Theseus could feel a

shiver in the stone walls around him, as if they longed to move once again.

He held out his free hand to Ariadne. "We don't want to get separated."

She eyed his outstretched hand for a moment before she slid her fingers to clasp his. She had a surprisingly strong grip, her fingers calloused.

Why did his heart pound harder at the touch of her hand in his? As if her nearness did something to him inside.

As they strode down the tunnel, their footsteps echoed against the stones. The torch crackled and popped.

It was too silent. Perhaps it would be wiser to remain alert, but Theseus couldn't help glancing back at Ariadne. "Can you tell me anything about this monster?"

"Not much." Ariadne shrugged. "Are you worried?"

"Just wondering what I should be looking for. A giant snake. A basilisk. A cockatrice. A bad bowl of porridge." Theseus peeked around a corner before he passed the tunnel branching to their left.

Ariadne gave a small snort of laughter. "Nothing as terrible as a bad bowl of porridge. I've heard the monster has horns."

Horns. That would make this an interesting fight. Theseus wracked his memory, trying to come up with a list of monsters with horns. There were quite a few, though the fact that the monster had to be small enough to fit inside the labyrinth narrowed the list somewhat. Was it a giant bull? A horned snake? A chimera?

Theseus glanced over his shoulder again. "Tell me. What brought you to the Court of Swordmaidens?"

"I was born to a former swordmaiden, though I grew up in the Court of Sand." Ariadne's shrug tugged on his hand. She was looking back as she twisted her hand to let out another loop of the magical yarn from its ball. "I always knew I would come here eventually."

"A former swordmaiden?" Theseus glanced around as they entered another intersection with seven branching tunnels. He kept going straight through to the center one.

Ariadne's hand briefly stilled on the yarn before she twisted it to unloop another section of the magical thread. "There is no place on this island for a married swordmaiden since men are forbidden to live here. My mother had to leave when her hand was won by my father."

Theseus halted so suddenly that Ariadne crashed into his back. He glanced over his shoulder at her, his mind churning.

If a married swordmaiden was forced to leave their Court, what would that mean for Queen Hippolyta if he won her hand? Was this a tradition of their Court that the married women had to leave, or was it merely a result of the tradition that men could not live on their island?

If it was the former, then his plan had been flawed from the beginning. Even if he won Hippolyta's hand, she would lose her crown and her Court, and he would have a wife without any warriors to save the Great Library, unless the new queen felt enough fealty for her former queen to still aid them.

But if it was the latter, then he still had a chance. Thanks to the Grand Hall of Anywhere Doors, travel between the Court of Knowledge and the Court of Swordmaidens was as simple as stepping through a Door. Surely, if he married Queen Hippolyta, they could both remain rulers of their respective Courts with the Anywhere Door to connect them. It would, after all, be more an arranged marriage than one of love.

Still, the thought niggled, along with the gaps in Ariadne's story. If she had been born to a former swordmaiden and presumably had trained from the moment she had been big enough to hold a sword, then why was she a servant?

By the way she wore the sword at her hip, she clearly had training. She moved with the confident grace of the warrior. He had always put that down to the fact that even the servants were highly trained here in this Court. Maybe she simply didn't enjoy her training enough to wish to be a swordmaiden and was content to remain a servant.

Yet that didn't fit with the fearless way she marched into this labyrinth at his side to face this monster. Nor with the fierce glimmer he caught in her eyes before she could hide it.

He shook himself, forcing the thoughts to the back of his mind. They were traipsing through a dangerous labyrinth searching for a monster to kill, after all. They had more important things to worry about right then.

"What about you? How did you become such a young king?" Ariadne flicked a glance at him before she turned her attention back to the ball of yarn.

In front of them, the passageway shuddered, then turned into three passageways instead of a single opening.

Once again he marched down the center tunnel as he tried to think of a way to answer. "My parents were killed in a monster attack. The monsters have been getting worse each Midsummer, and the Court of Knowledge can no longer handle them on our own. We aren't a Court of warriors."

"Thus your desperation to marry Queen Hippolyta." Ariadne's voice remained neutral, not giving away her thoughts on the matter.

Theseus was here to win Queen Hippolyta's hand. Then why did Ariadne's hand feel so right in his? Why was it so easy to talk with her?

"I need to save my Court from more death and suffering." Theseus couldn't help but clasp her hand tighter, even knowing he would soon be forced to let her go. "This Midsummer Night looks to be the worst we've seen in a long, long time. My Court and the Great Library won't survive without help."

"I am sorry." Ariadne's voice was soft, carrying a trace of pain as if she understood the depth of love for a Court that would cause him to sacrifice himself to save it.

He opened his mouth, but a distant sound drifted from the darkness of the tunnel ahead of them.

He halted, and this time Ariadne stopped when he did. She tensed, her stance shifting to that of a warrior prepared to do battle.

Theseus tilted his head, listening. There. A shuffling of heavy footsteps accompanied by a metal clanking. He let go of Ariadne's hand, switched the torch to that hand, and drew his sword.

As he stalked down the tunnel, Ariadne fell into step behind him, still trailing the yarn with one hand and now also gripping her sword.

Theseus probably shouldn't feel so reassured, having her at his back. She was probably just as much his enemy as the monster he was about to face. But her steady stride and assured grip on her sword were exactly what he would have dreamed for a wife at his side.

He shook himself. No time to think about that. Nor would he be marrying the servant girl behind him, no matter what his heart was whispering to him. He was here to win the hand of her cold, hard-eyed queen.

A light was coming from around a corner of the tunnel. Theseus snuffed the torch and gently set it on the floor.

As he crept closer to the corner, the clanking and shuffling grew louder. A shadow of some horned monster took shape across the wall in front of him. Its shadow was tall, stretching far above Theseus's head until the tips of its wide, bull's horns spread onto the ceiling of the passageway. Its broad shoulders were muscular even in shadow.

He glanced over his shoulder at Ariadne and whispered, "Thank you for your help. While I trust that you are skilled with that sword, I think this fight is one I need to face alone."

Ariadne nodded, her mouth pressing into a tight line. She had given him far more help than she probably should have, considering this was the first of his trials to win the hand of her queen. But she understood as much as he did that, when it came to the actual monster battle, he could accept no help if he were to pass the test.

Raising his sword, he drew in a deep breath, then charged forward. As he rounded the corner in the tunnel, he found himself in a small square chamber.

In the center of the chamber stood a goblin woman. She was a head taller than Theseus with large branching horns sticking from either side of her head. She had just the hint of a cow's muzzle while her light brown hair flowed around her horns and down her back. Her leather tunic was sleeveless, showing off her muscled arms.

She was not, however, a monster. Nor was she armed, besides her fists that looked capable of knocking Theseus's head in. When she moved, a chain rattled, attached to the wall on one end and a shackle around her ankle on the other.

Theseus lowered his sword, heat burning from his chest up to his head. While some fae had prejudices against the goblinkind, the goblins were not monsters. Monsters were mere soulless creatures while goblins were people as much as Theseus or the talking horses or the Great Dragons, who were different than the mere creature dragons.

Theseus had thought Queen Hippolyta was not one who held such prejudices against the goblins, but apparently, he had been wrong. If this was how she treated a goblin woman, then Theseus had no wish to win her hand. He would find some other way to save his Court.

He lowered his sword and held out his other hand, palm up. "I won't hurt you. I'm here to rescue you."

The woman's gaze flicked past Theseus toward Ariadne behind him. Just for a moment, but Theseus still noted it to examine later.

When the cow-headed goblin woman focused on Theseus again, she nodded, and her stance relaxed.

"Hold still, and I'll cut your chains." Theseus stepped forward, his jaw clenched so hard it hurt. This was despicable, keeping a woman chained like a monster deep in this labyrinth. He swung his sword, the blade slicing through the chains easily.

Strange, that. These chains weren't the strong faerie steel of the dungeon chains waiting for him back at Hippolyta's palace. Instead, these were an inferior metal, one that his sword could cut without effort.

Another thing to mull over later. As the past three days had proven, he would have plenty of time to himself once he finished this task.

He sheathed his sword with a snap and marched past Ariadne, gesturing for the two women to follow him. "Come. I need to have a word with your queen."

After a moment, he could hear their two sets of footsteps trailing after him, though he didn't pause to glance at them. He trailed his fingers along the golden string, its glow enough to light his way even without a torch. The yarn shuddered, and Ariadne must be rewinding it as she and the goblin woman followed him.

As they reached the labyrinth's exit, Theseus stalked into the light, blinking at the brightness of the midday sun, before he marched over to Queen Hippolyta's impassive, imposing form, gesturing behind him. "What is the meaning of this? This woman is no monster. I had thought the Court of Swordmaidens was above such prejudices, but it seems I was mistaken. How dare you keep one of the goblinkind chained inside that labyrinth!"

Queen Hippolyta swept her gaze past Theseus, as if dismissing him as inconsequential. "Thank you for your service in this test, Minnie. You may go with the compliments of your queen."

Theseus shot a glance over his shoulder as the goblin woman—Minnie, presumably—bowed and strode off. As she walked, she pulled a key out of her pocket. She halted for a moment to unlock the shackle from her ankle before she set out again, key in one hand, shackle swinging from the other.

A test. But not the one he had thought it was. This had never been a test of his ability to navigate the labyrinth or kill a monster. This trial was designed to reveal his prejudices and how he would react to an injustice.

Turning back to him, Queen Hippolyta raised her eyebrows, her gaze so cold it was surprising that he didn't freeze where he stood. "King Theseus, do you know nothing of my Court? The Court of Swordmaidens is a refuge for women of all the Courts of the Fae Realm, including those from the Goblin Court. You have failed to recognize the true purpose of the Court of Swordmaidens. Guards, please escort him back to his dungeon cell."

Theseus didn't resist as the swordmaidens gripped his arms and dragged him back toward the palace balanced high on the cliffs above them.

Chapter Four

Theseus slumped against the wall in his cell, hands pinned above his head by his chains.

Had he passed that test? Or failed? He couldn't be sure.

Sure, he had recognized that Minnie wasn't a monster. He proved that he didn't hold the prejudices of some of the other Court rulers.

But he hadn't realized that her presence there was a part of the test. Of course Hippolyta wouldn't lock up one of her own in the labyrinth. He would have realized that, if he had stopped to think it through. Instead, he'd been so angry at the sight of Minnie chained deep in the labyrinth—a cell even worse than the dungeon where he once again found himself—that he hadn't paused to think. In that, he had failed.

What would have happened if he'd actually attacked Minnie? The goblin woman was strong. But would her bare hands have been enough to stop his sword?

Maybe. Still, that seemed like quite the risk, especially

considering the chain around her ankle would hamper her maneuverability. She wouldn't have time to pause and free herself if he attacked.

He squeezed his eyes shut, once again seeing Ariadne drawing her sword, her golden hair gleaming in the torchlight.

Ariadne had been in on it the whole time. She hadn't been there to help him, despite her golden string. She was there to protect Minnie, should Theseus prove to be the kind to attack her. Her drawn sword had been for Theseus, not the so-called monster.

And like a fool, he had given her his undefended back. She could have run him through whenever she wished. Was it a good sign for his chances that she hadn't?

It confirmed his suspicions that Ariadne was no mere serving woman. She must be a swordmaiden herself, someone that Queen Hippolyta trusted implicitly for a mission like that.

As expected, the light patter of her footsteps sounded on the stairs a few moments before she came into view, carrying his supper tray as always.

Theseus leaned his head against the stone wall behind him. "You don't have to pretend anymore."

Ariadne froze, one hand balancing his tray of food, the other reaching for the ring of keys at her belt. A blank expression slammed across her face. "I don't?"

"I know you're a swordmaiden. Clearly a high-ranking swordmaiden, trusted by Queen Hippolyta." Theseus searched Ariadne's face for her reaction.

The blank expression cleared, something almost like relief slumping her shoulders for a moment before she straightened. Her gaze focused on her hand rather than on him as she twisted the key in the lock. "I wondered how long it would take you to put the pieces together."

Something in her reaction seemed off, though he couldn't name what it was. He filed it away to ponder once he was alone in the dungeon cell again.

"It took far longer than it should have." Theseus kept his tone light as she sat on the floor across from him.

She grinned, the light back in her clear blue eyes. "A pitiful performance for the king of the Court of Knowledge. Aren't you supposed to be intelligent?"

He pulled himself into a kneeling position and took the plate she offered him, holding it level with his nose. "Knowledgeable, yes. Intelligent, maybe. Wise, not necessarily."

She snorted a laugh. Not a tinkling, pretty laugh. But a snorting, loud laugh that sounded like she would choke on her own spit at any moment. "True. If you were wise, you wouldn't be here."

"Perhaps. But I'm desperate." He shrugged and swung the plate of food in front of his face. With his hands chained as they were, he swiveled his hands at the end of the chain to shovel the food from the plate directly into his mouth. It wasn't elegant, but it worked.

Funny how Queen Hippolyta claimed she would never chain Minnie, but she had no problem keeping Theseus in chains. Perhaps it was all a part of his test, but it still rankled.

He finished the plate of greens and fruit and held out the empty plate to Ariadne. "So, the golden string. Did we actually need it? Or would you have been able to navigate the labyrinth without it?"

"We needed it." Ariadne shrugged, then swapped out the plate for a slice of bread. "The labyrinth is tricky. It is very easy to find your way deep inside it, but very difficult to find your way out. The labyrinth would have taken us to Minnie eventually, but it would have made it very difficult to leave without the golden yarn."

Ah. The labyrinth was one of *those* kinds of enchanted mazes. It was a good thing he'd had Ariadne with him. It would have been far more difficult if he'd been by himself.

"Well, for all your trickery, I am thankful you showed up with that magic yarn." Theseus spoke between bites of his bread before he gestured to her with the crust. "Getting lost in a labyrinth would not have helped my Court any. If your queen wants some real monsters for her labyrinth, I can send a few her way on Midsummer Night. I have a feeling my Court will have more than enough to spare."

"She might be willing to take you up on that, you know." Ariadne's gaze searched his face, as if her words were yet another test. "We swordmaidens always appreciate a good fight."

Was she trying to tell him that he didn't need to win Hippolyta's hand in order to secure the help of the swordmaidens? That Queen Hippolyta would be willing to bargain with him for their help without a marriage involved?

Perhaps. Maybe that had been what she had been getting at when she'd asked him what the Court of

Knowledge had to offer the Court of Swordmaidens. She had wanted a bargain, not a marriage.

But as her reaction to his answer had shown, he didn't have anything to offer the Court of Swordmaidens. Nothing that they seemed to want and nothing that he was willing to give. He could not risk giving the Court of Swordmaidens too much power over the Court of Knowledge, if he made a bargain that was less than balanced.

He couldn't bargain. Marriage it would have to be.

Ariadne's smile faded, and she set the tray with plates aside. She pulled out a folded piece of paper from where it had been tucked underneath her belt. "A note came from your steward."

Theseus reached as far forward as he could against the chains to take the paper from her. Unfolding it, he quickly read the note, written in Philostrate's familiar handwriting.

The news from his Court wasn't good. A few monsters had already slipped through the barrier between realms and hurt several people before the monsters were dispatched. Thankfully there had been no fatalities, but it was only a matter of time.

To add to the problems, King Oberon and Queen Titania's fighting was escalating to the point that the Court of Revels was starting to split as its members took sides.

It just reinforced that he had to see this through. He had to win the hand of Queen Hippolyta and save his Court.

"It must be serious." Ariadne's expression remained

impassive, though she probably knew what the note said already since Theseus assumed the swordmaidens would have read his message before giving it to him.

"Midsummer is just growing more dangerous back in my Court. There was a monster attack, and some of my people were injured." Theseus let out a long sigh and tucked the note into a pocket of his shirt.

"You must love your Court very much." Ariadne's voice was soft, her light blue eyes gentling in a way he hadn't seen before.

"Yes." Theseus forced himself to smile and bring back the lighthearted tone of a moment ago. "I'm here, aren't I? I'm clearly desperate."

Ariadne's mouth twitched, as if she wanted to smirk but didn't allow herself that freedom. "You've told me a lot about the Library. Do you live in the Library itself?"

"No, the castle is connected to the Library by the Grand Hall of Anywhere Doors." Theseus flexed his fingers in the shackles. They were tingling from being pinned above his head for so long. He would have to stand for a while soon to let the blood flow back into his hands. "But the castle and the Library share much of the same architecture."

"What is it like?" Ariadne's keen gaze did something to him, and it started him talking. Once he did, he found himself telling her all about the palace. What it was like growing up there. Stories of himself when he was little and getting into trouble. Mostly by hiding away somewhere deep inside the Library, reading when he was supposed to be doing something else.

She shared her own stories about her early years in the

Court of Sand. It sounded like a hard life in that Court, but a good one.

"Are your parents still alive?" Theseus was standing now, leaning against the wall with his hands at his sides.

"Yes. They still live in the Court of Sand, along with my two brothers and my sister. She didn't want to join the Court of Swordmaidens the way I did." Ariadne's gaze dropped, her tone carrying an edge of pain.

It must be hard, leaving her family at such a young age to join the Court of Swordmaidens. How free was Ariadne to visit her family? Her father and brothers wouldn't be welcome to visit her at her Court.

It itched at him. Yet another thing to think on when Ariadne left him alone once more.

Not that Theseus wanted her to leave anytime soon. He would happily talk with her long into the night. It hurt, knowing he shouldn't enjoy her company this much. He was planning to win the hand of Hippolyta.

But this swordmaiden before him was already well on her way to stealing his heart.

Chapter Five

O nce again, Theseus stood between two swordmaidens, waiting for Queen Hippolyta's next task. The morning sunlight twinkled on the ocean waves as they washed against the island's cliffs. The palace and cluster of stone homes filled the point of land behind him while a tree-covered island wilderness spread out before him. A warm breeze stirred his hair, keeping the heat of the day from being too unbearable.

If the day was warm, Queen Hippolyta was doing her best to cool it down with the ice in her eyes. "King Theseus. A giant pig is currently ravaging our island. Your second task is to capture the pig."

"That's it? No underhanded tests or trying to trick me into killing someone?" Theseus crossed his arms, glaring right back.

Queen Hippolyta raised a single eyebrow, as if to tell him that it wouldn't be a test if she gave him the answer. "You have until sundown."

One of the swordmaidens shoved a rope at him. When he took it, both swordmaidens gave him a push toward the uninhabited wild section of the island before him.

He could take the hint. Without a glance over his shoulder at the swordmaiden queen, he strolled forward. The shadows beneath the trees enfolded him as the undergrowth scraped against his arms and legs. He had to fight his way between the plants, battling for every step, until he stepped into a section of forest with taller trees, their foliage shading the forest floor so completely that very little undergrowth could flourish.

Ariadne leaned against one of the nearby trees, still dressed in her white servant's garb despite the fact that he knew the truth.

He halted in front of her, hefting the rope higher on his shoulder. "Do you have any magic items to help with my task today? A golden lasso or a magic apple to lure the pig into a trap?"

Ariadne smirked, an expression that seemed more confident than the smiles she had given him before. Perhaps she felt free to be herself, now that she wasn't lying about being a servant. "Nope. For this task, you are on your own."

"Will you at least keep me company?" Theseus gestured at the forest around them. "This is a small island, but it still might take a while to locate this pig."

"Of course. After all, who could resist your charm." She raised her eyebrows to match the sarcasm in her words.

It made him want to take as long as possible to round

up this rampaging pig. Spending the day tromping across this beautiful island with her at his side sounded like a pleasant way to pass time. Besides, he likely would never have another chance to explore this island, considering the rule against men. Win or lose, he would be banished from this island forever once these trials were over.

He set off deeper into the forest, and Ariadne fell into step with him. Or, at least, as much as she could as they wound their way between trees and pushed through stands of thick undergrowth.

After a few minutes, Theseus stumbled from the brush onto a pebbled path. He glanced up and down the path, sighing when the left side of the path paralleled the thick forest he had been fighting his way through.

He pointed at the path. "You could have mentioned that there was an easier way."

Ariadne smirked, brushing dirt and leaves from her white dress. "Where would be the fun in that? This is supposed to be a trial, after all, not an easy stroll."

She had a point, but he wasn't going to let it go that easily, even if he wasn't truly angry. "Is there anything wrong with following the path now?"

Her smirk didn't falter. If anything, her eyes twinkled more.

Not a good sign. Would the swordmaidens lay traps on the trails on their island?

Wrong question. Of course they would. The better questions would be, what kind of traps had they laid and how could he spot them?

"What should I look out for?"

"The usual. A few trip wires, hidden pits with spikes

at the bottom, swinging logs. That sort of thing." Ariadne shrugged, as if strolling down a trail littered with deadly snares wasn't a big deal.

Theseus didn't dare even shuffle his feet, knowing how dangerous this was. And he had been blithely bumbling through the forest a moment ago. Was the forest as deadly as the path? He twisted to better face Ariadne while keeping his feet planted where they were. "If I asked nicely, would you warn me before I step into any traps?"

"Maybe. Maybe not." Ariadne started off down the path deeper into the island.

It wasn't the most reassuring answer. But Theseus hurried after her, trying to step where she stepped and move when she moved. When she switched to walking on the far left side of the path, he did the same. When she stepped higher, he did too, barely spotting the thin trip wire as he cleared it.

She strode with such purpose and ease that he suspected the swordmaidens must train frequently along this path. Perhaps they took it at a full run, each snare memorized through practice.

After about a mile of walking, taking several branching paths, Ariadne halted. As she did, Theseus also heard the snuffling, grunting, squealing sounds from ahead.

The undergrowth shook before a massive animal burst from the trees. It was covered in dark gray, wiry fur with gleaming tusks curving out of either side of its mouth. Its sloping back was as tall as Theseus was, its head level with his chest and so large that his torso would fit inside its mouth.

That mouth gaped open, showing jagged teeth, as the giant pig bellowed. Still bellowing, it charged straight at Ariadne and Theseus.

Ariadne dove from the path, and Theseus threw himself after her a heartbeat later. He rolled, scrambling behind a large rock. The ground shuddered as the giant pig thundered past. It plowed right through a trip wire, and a log swung from the forest and bumped into the pig's side. The pig squealed but didn't slow.

Theseus touched the rope he still had slung over his shoulder. "Queen Hippolyta gave me this rope as a joke, didn't she? It isn't going to do much against that monster. A magic lasso would be rather useful right now."

Ariadne peeked over the rock, grimacing. "Sorry. No magic rope."

Even if Theseus managed to get this rope around the pig's neck, that creature was stronger and heavier than he was and would drag him all over the forest until his skin was stripped from his body. Not a pleasant way to die.

That meant he needed another plan.

He peered over the rock alongside Ariadne. The pig seemingly had forgotten them and crashed about the brush, tearing up saplings and trampling ferns.

What had caused the creature to become so angry? Perhaps it was merely a monster, bent on destroying everything and everyone in its path. But usually monsters targeted people, hunting them down wherever they could find them. Yet this pig was largely ignoring them, except for the moment when they had drawn its attention.

A creature—a monstrous creature, even—but not truly a monster from the Realm of Monsters.

Then what was causing this giant pig to go on a rampage? Animals normally didn't carry this kind of sustained anger, though wild pigs were known to be more ornery than most.

What Theseus wouldn't give for a few hours to consult with the Great Library. The librarians there would have all the information he would need within a few minutes if he asked. How was he supposed to come up with a proper plan without that information at his fingertips?

As the giant pig thrashed through the brush closer to them, Theseus studied it as closely as he could manage while the animal bellowed and charged random trees. If he couldn't research at the Great Library, then he would have to go with good old-fashioned observation.

There wasn't much to see. It was a standard wild pig. Dark bristles. Tusks. Chunky body. Just really, really huge.

Except...Theseus squinted to focus. That pig was a sow. "That's a female pig."

"Of course. This is the Island of Swordmaidens." Ariadne raised her eyebrows at him.

"Yes, but that pig is a mother." Something that was rather obvious, based on the way its body was swollen from feeding piglets. "Which I know for a fact can't happen without a male pig being around, at least for a little while."

Ariadne shrugged. "It is still free to come and go as it chooses."

He wasn't sure he wanted to know how this giant pig would get on and off the island.

As he kept an eye on the pig, its tail lifted and something golden popped out and dropped to the ground.

He glanced at Ariadne. "The pig poops gold."

As if this day wasn't already weird enough.

"It's a giant pig. Obviously it's magical." Ariadne pointed at the pig, though she kept her hand low to avoid the pig seeing them.

Ah, so this was part of the test. The temptation to catch the pig and keep it for himself rather than turn it over to Queen Hippolyta.

Another bellow came from the pig as it plowed down yet another tree. Theseus flinched and ducked lower behind the rock. He didn't care if this pig pooped gold, diamonds, and rubies. No way was he keeping that creature for himself.

He turned back to the giant sow and studied it again. It was alone, even though it must have piglets young enough to need care.

That was why it was so angry. It was separated from its young.

If he couldn't rope and drag this gigantic pig back to its piglets, then perhaps he could use one of the piglets to lure it back to its pen, wherever that was.

"Can you show me its pen and piglets?" Theseus eased down into hiding behind the rock, glancing at Ariadne.

"Yes. Follow me." Ariadne crawled backwards deeper into the brush before she stood.

If she agreed so easily, then finding the pen wasn't the test, even if figuring out that this sow had piglets seemed to be part of it.

Theseus matched Ariadne's movements, working to stay quiet to avoid attracting the attention of the enraged pig once again.

Once they were out of sight of the pig—though they could still hear its distant bellows and squeals—Ariadne returned to the path.

The trail sloped upward, leaving the forest as it climbed into a rocky section of the island. Finally, they arrived at the mouth of a canyon surrounded by steep cliffs on all but one side. This final side had a large timber stockade taller than Theseus built across it. A wooden gate was locked with a bar the size of a small tree.

No part of the fence or gate was damaged. It was even still locked.

That meant the pig hadn't gotten away on its own. It had been purposely released and driven into the forest as part of this test.

Theseus caught Ariadne glancing at him, something in her gaze pointed. Did she want him to read into this situation? It seemed cruel to drive a mother pig away from its young.

He would think about it later. Right now, the priority was reuniting the giant sow with its piglets.

Reaching the gate, he gripped one end of the locking bar. "Could you please lift the other end?"

Ariadne lifted her end of the locking bar without

apparent effort as Theseus heaved his end free of its bracket. They lowered the bar to the ground where it wouldn't be in the way.

Theseus yanked open the large gate and stepped inside the pigpen.

The smell hit him first. Apparently even magical pigs had that same rancid manure stench as regular pigs. A brown slurry spread out in front of him, veined with gold streaks.

Five piglets splashed about in the muck, occasionally squealing and grunting as if they were looking for their mother and were worried that they couldn't find her. Their brown fur appeared softer than the wiry texture of their mother's coat, and stripes of lighter fur lined their backs. They might have been cute, if they hadn't been so big they reached his knees and probably weighed fifty or sixty pounds.

As he stood there, gaping, one of the piglets pooped out a stream of gold.

His stomach churned. He didn't know who would be desperate enough to collect that gold, but he certainly wasn't.

Though with this much gold, he would have leverage. He could bargain with any Court he wished, giving them gold in exchange for the use of their warriors on Midsummer Night. He wouldn't have to marry Hippolyta or continue these trials.

It would be easy enough to carry off one of these piglets and head straight for the Anywhere Door. This gold could be a far more certain salvation than risking the future of his Court on his success in these trials.

He shook himself. What was he thinking? He'd never thought himself the type to be tempted by the lure of gold, but it turned out he was desperate enough to think about it.

It was a foolish thought. If he stole away a piglet, the Court of Swordmaidens would come after him, and adding a war with the Court of Swordmaidens onto the chaos of the upcoming Midsummer Night would doubly doom his Court.

Even assuming the swordmaidens let him get away with it, the piglet would likely die, separated from its mother so young. Besides, magic like this was tricky. He didn't know why these pigs pooped gold. It might be something they ate or something about the magic of this island. He couldn't be sure the piglet would still poop gold if taken from its habitat.

No, he needed to concentrate on finishing this task. He wouldn't fail, and he would win Queen Hippolyta's hand.

Chapter Six

Facing the piglets, Theseus took the rope off his shoulder. "I take it capturing a piglet isn't something with which you will help me."

Ariadne rolled her eyes and gestured down at her white dress. After tromping through the forest, it was streaked with green plant stains and coated with dirt along the hem. "In this dress? Of course not. I intend to stand here and laugh while you get coated in manure and mud."

"So glad I can provide your entertainment for the day." Theseus grimaced as he took a step forward and his boots sank into the slop all the way past his ankles. It took effort to pull his foot free, the mud making a sucking sound, as he trudged another step. "Now I understand why you tagged along. It wasn't to help but to enjoy my muddy humiliation."

Ariadne smirked as she swung the gate closed, standing in front of it. At least she would make sure none of the piglets escaped, since the gate couldn't be locked from the inside.

Theseus lumbered several more glopping steps deeper into the pigpen as he formed a loop at the end of the rope. He had some vague notion of how to snag something with a rope, but he'd never done it himself. It wasn't like he had a great need to wrangle pigs as the king of a library.

As he neared, the piglets scattered with a squeal, running in all different directions. He threw the rope, and the loop plopped in the mud after flying a laughably short distance nowhere near any of the piglets.

Yep, just as terrible as he'd feared.

He trudged back to Ariadne, dragging the end of the rope behind him, and dropped the rope beside her. It would be more trouble than it would be worth. With his lack of skill, he would be better off just grabbing a piglet with his bare hands, then popping the rope over its head afterwards.

She didn't say anything about his ditching the rope. Instead, she crossed her arms and leaned against the stockade next to the gate, her mouth twitching as if she were trying and failing to hold back her grin.

Facing the piglets, Theseus waded into the slop once again. The leather of his boots grew soaked until wetness squished between his toes with each step.

He tiptoed closer to one of the piglets, trying to get as close as possible.

The piglet looked up, and he dove. His hands brushed along the piglet's furry back before it slipped out of his grasp.

Theseus landed in the mud with a splat. Mud squished through his clothes and splashed onto his face. He spat, shuddering as he pushed himself onto his hands and knees.

After this was over, he would have to beg on hands and knees for Queen Hippolyta to send a message to Philostrate, asking for a fresh set of clothes. What he was wearing had already been growing rank after six days in the dungeon. The towel and bowl of water he had been given to wash every three days had been barely enough to wash himself, not his clothes.

Ariadne's snorting laugh rang out behind him.

He shoved to his feet and raced after the piglets, slipping and sliding and falling into the mud. He tried to tackle another piglet and once again fell face-first in the muck.

As he pushed onto his elbows, he panted as he swiped mud from his face. This wasn't working. He wasn't fast enough to outrun or outmaneuver the piglets.

He glanced over his shoulder. The sun was already past noon. He was running out of time.

Theseus rolled into a sitting position in the mud. At this point, he was already covered head-to-toe. More mud didn't matter.

Chasing the piglets just riled them up. Like any animal, he needed calm and patience and stillness to lure them into ignoring him.

For a few minutes, the piglets continued to squeal and race around. But as Theseus remained still and silent, the piglets calmed and went back to snuffling in the mud.

He stayed frozen sitting in the mud, all but holding

his breath as one of the piglets wandered closer and closer toward him.

The piglet nipped at his knees, its still toothless gums knocking against his kneecap.

Theseus lunged and wrapped his arms around the piglet's middle. The piglet let out a squeal and squirmed, nearly shooting right out of his grasp. He tightened his arms around the piglet's waist and hung on as the piglet dragged him through the mud.

With a twist, he managed to knock the piglet off its feet. Theseus scrambled to get his feet under him, and as he stood, he hefted the piglet. Its hooves flailed, kicking Theseus's ribs and legs. He winced at the sharp scrape of the hooves even through his mud-coated clothing.

He hurried through the mud toward Ariadne and the rope at her feet. As he neared, he adjusted his grip on the squirming piglet. "Could you put the rope on him? Or is that helping me too much?"

Ariadne snorted a laugh as she picked up the rope. She leaned out to slide the rope over the piglet's head, then past his front legs to keep him from just slipping out of it again. She moved gingerly, as if trying to avoid brushing against the muck liberally coating both him and the piglet.

Once the loop was tightened, Theseus set down the pig, rubbing at his ribs. He took the rope from Ariadne, gripping it tightly as the piglet lunged at the end of the rope, trying to escape. "I'm going to go lure the sow back here. Would you mind waiting here to open the gate for me?"

"I can do that." Ariadne's light blue eyes studied him, as if searching for the truth of his words.

If he was going to give in to the temptation to steal a gold-pooping pig, then this was his chance. He had a captured piglet. Instead of tracking down the sow, he could head for the Anywhere Door instead.

Even if he had entertained such a temptation before, chasing down this piglet had cured him of that urge. At this point, he just wanted to get that sow back with its babies as quickly as possible and be done with the disgusting creatures.

He held her gaze. "I'll be back. And I'll be coming in fast, so be ready with the gate."

He had to lean his weight into the rope to drag the piglet through the gate and down the path. The piglet dug in its heels, then dashed in one direction until it hit the end of the rope hard enough to cause Theseus to stumble a step before he caught himself.

By the time he'd gone a few yards down the trail, his arms ached from the constant tugging. Still, it was better than carrying the piglet the whole way.

Sooner than he'd expected, he heard snorting and crashing in the forest ahead. He picked up the piglet, grimacing at its weight. He juggled both the piglet and the coils of rope as the piglet flailed and let out a loud squeal.

An answering, deeper squeal came from the forest ahead of him.

Time to go. Theseus spun on his heel and raced back the way he'd come as quickly as he could while hefting a fifty-pound piglet in his arms.

The crashing turned in his direction, the ground shaking beneath him. A bellow roared behind him, far too close.

The path sloped up hill. Theseus gritted his teeth and leaned into each stride. The piglet in his arms squealed and flailed wildly now that its mother was in sight.

If Theseus slipped, that giant pig would be on him in a second. He could almost feel its hot breath on the back of his neck.

The stockade rose into view, wedging between the cliffs on either side of the valley. Theseus dug for the last strength in his legs to sprint the last few yards as he shouted, "Ariadne! The gate!"

She was already swinging it open, her eyes widening as her gaze fixed on something behind him.

He didn't dare turn and look. At the gate, he chucked the piglet as hard and far as he could, the baby animal squealing as it flew through the air. The rope slithered to the ground, falling off the piglet.

He didn't see the piglet land, as he was already rolling out of the way, though he knew the sloppy mud would cushion the landing and keep the piglet from harm.

The ground shuddered as the giant sow thundered by in a blur of dark fur, gleaming tusks, and flashing hooves.

By the time Theseus scrambled to his feet, Ariadne was shoving the gate closed. He joined her, and together they slammed it closed and hefted the locking bar into place.

Once the gate was securely closed, Theseus sagged against the wood, still huffing panting breaths. "Was that as close as I thought it was?"

"Closer." Ariadne leaned against the stockade next to him. "I thought you were pig-bait for sure."

"What a way to go. Trampled by a giant pig." Theseus rested his head against the stockade. "King Oberon never would have let my successor forget that I had been killed off in such a manner."

"Another reason to be glad you weren't killed." Ariadne grimaced. "Anything that gives King Oberon of the Court of Revels a reason to gloat should be avoided."

The mother pig's satisfied grunting came from inside the stockade, answered by higher pitched grunts by the piglets.

Theseus pushed away from the stockade, then peered between two of the large logs. The sow wallowed deep in the mud, the five piglets clustering around her.

"I see you have completed your task, King Theseus."

He spun at the cold tone of Queen Hippolyta's voice behind him. She stood on the trail, flanked by a cadre of eight swordmaidens.

"Yes. I have returned the mother pig to where she belongs." Theseus plucked at his clothes. Dried mud flaked off and rained to the ground. "Please tell me my reward for succeeding in this task will be a bath."

"The ocean is that way." Queen Hippolyta jabbed her finger toward the horizon past the stockade, where the rocks ended in a cliff, giving a view of nothing but sky.

Theseus grimaced. He could tell even from there that the cliff would be far too high for a jump into the ocean.

It seemed he would be stuck wallowing in pig manure. That would make his dungeon cell so pleasant.

Even the breeze through the barred window wouldn't be enough to whisk away this stench.

THESEUS PACED AS MUCH as he could inside his cell, swinging his arms to get as much airflow to his clothes as possible.

He was still dripping seawater and mud onto the floor of his cell. At least Queen Hippolyta had allowed him to take a detour to the beach and attempt to wash the mud off himself and his clothes all in one go. He was now gritty with both drying salt from the seawater and the ground-in pig muck he hadn't been able to scrub away in the hurried dousing.

The expected footsteps padded on the stairs a moment before Ariadne appeared, carrying a bundle of clothing and a towel. Another woman dressed in white carried a bowl and pitcher, presumably filled with water.

"Oh, good." Theseus slumped against the wall. "Please tell me those clothes are for me."

"Your steward Philostrate kindly sent clothes when he was alerted that you needed a fresh set." Ariadne unlocked his cell door. She waved for the other servant woman to step in first.

The servant woman scurried inside, set the bowl and pitcher on the floor out of Theseus's reach, then swiftly left, hurrying back up the stairs.

Ariadne set her bundle of clothes and the towel on the floor next to the pitcher.

Theseus held out his wrists. "I promise I won't try anything."

"I wasn't worried." Ariadne smirked as she unlocked the shackles around his ankles. She stood and reached for his hand. She unlocked first one manacle, then the other, letting them fall to clank against the stone wall. "You'd better hurry. You have ten minutes."

She strolled out of his cell, shutting and locking the door behind her. She disappeared around the corner, but then her footsteps halted.

"Aren't you going to leave?" Theseus peeled off his mud-covered shirt and dropped it to the floor well away from the clean clothes.

"Just be glad I'm standing out of sight and giving you that much privacy," Ariadne called back, her voice coming from what Theseus guessed was the base of the stairs.

"Thank you for that consideration." Theseus hurriedly stripped out of his foul clothes, washed, and put on the new clothing.

He was lacing up his boots when Ariadne reappeared, her mouth pressed tight against a grin. He straightened. "When you said ten minutes, you meant ten minutes and not a second more."

"More than sufficient time, unless you're the type given to preening." She raised her eyebrow as she let herself into his cell.

He obligingly held out his hands.

As she clapped the manacle around his wrist, her fingers brushed against his skin.

Theseus stilled as he caught a whiff of the fresh, floral

scent wafting from her hair. His skin tingled from her touch as he grew all too aware of her nearness.

It would be easy to close the distance and kiss her smirking mouth. He found himself swaying closer, the temptation churning inside him.

The second manacle clicked closed around his other wrist, the faerie steel cold against his skin.

He jerked back, giving himself a mental shake. What was he thinking? He intended to win Queen Hippolyta's hand, not Ariadne's.

Could he ask for Ariadne's hand, instead of Queen Hippolyta's, at the end of this? She was a trusted swordmaiden, for all that she still dressed like a servant.

Was she high enough in the ranks of the swordmaidens that she could ask for help for Theseus's Court, if she became its queen? Or would she be cut off from the swordmaidens, kicked off their island and out of their Court?

He couldn't let this attraction to Ariadne progress any further. For the sake of his Court, he had to marry Queen Hippolyta. It was the only way to guarantee the help of the swordmaidens.

"Ariadne, I..." He cleared his throat as she knelt to lock the shackles around his ankles once again.

"Yes?" She glanced up at him before turning her attention back to the chains.

What should he say? Did she even feel this same attraction that he did? Or would she just find it awkward if he said something? He coughed, his tongue all but stuck to the roof of his mouth. "Never mind."

Ariadne stood, grimacing as she gathered up his dirty

clothes and dumped them in the bowl half-filled with muddy water. She set the damp towel and empty pitcher on top before she picked up the whole bundle of stuff. She left his cell, locking his door behind her.

Theseus gathered his thoughts, his chest tight. "Ariadne?"

She turned and raised her eyebrow again. "Finally found your tongue?"

He couldn't give in to the invitation to banter. "I have to win Queen Hippolyta's hand. It is too important to my Court."

He had expected hurt to flash across her eyes, her shoulders to slump, or perhaps even tears to form.

Instead, the corners of her mouth twitched, as if she was fighting a smirk. "I know."

With a swift, precise turn, she headed for the stairs. The last glimpse Theseus had was of her long blonde braid swinging across her back.

Chapter Seven

Theseus stood in the center of a colosseum. The sandy floor crunched beneath his feet. Sword-maidens and servants filled the tiers of benches formed of white stone. The black-haired, cold queen stared down at him from her dais.

He adjusted his grip on his sword's hilt, willing his palm to remain unsweaty. This was his final test, and he had no choice but to win. His Court's survival depended on his victory.

A door opened in the stone wall surrounding the combat arena. A figure dressed in leather combat armor sauntered toward him, her head high, her grip on her sword relaxed. Her golden hair was wound in many braids around her head, the braids studded with winking diamonds.

Ariadne.

Except...Theseus studied her more closely. Her swaggering confidence. Her smirk glinting in her eyes.

The pieces and hints he'd stashed away for thought fell into place with each step she took toward him.

The swordmaiden he had known as Ariadne halted in front of him, her mouth twisting into a smirk. "Well, King Theseus? Are you ready for your final trial?"

"It is an honor to fight you." Theseus held her gaze as he added, "Queen Hippolyta."

Her smirk widened, and she languidly swung her sword. "I am the queen of the Court of Swordmaidens. Of course I will be fighting for my own hand."

She glanced at the dais and nodded.

The fake Queen Hippolyta—most likely the real Ariadne—stood, then stepped aside, taking her place next to the throne as one of the queen's guards.

Theseus tightened his grip on his sword and faced Ariadne—no, Hippolyta. It had taken him far too long to realize the truth. But the signs had all been there. The way the servant he had known as Ariadne was clearly a swordmaiden in disguise. The time she spent with him each day, as if trying to get to know him. The way the fake Hippolyta had barely interacted with him. All the little tricks Hippolyta had played on him all along, each one yet another test, including hiding her identity.

He might have been angrier at all the trickery if he hadn't been so relieved to find that he had been fighting for her hand—not the hand of that cold-eyed swordmaiden—all along.

It would come down to this. His skill against hers.

He had no hope of truly beating her in a sword fight. She had, after all, dedicated her life to learning the ways of the sword and battle. He was the king of a court of librarians. While he had some training, it had not been his focus nor his purpose.

Would she let him win? Would she give him her hand? She knew how important this was for his Court. Surely she felt the same attraction that he did.

Hippolyta prowled in a circle around him in graceful strides. "I ask again, King Theseus. Are you ready? I will even let you call the start."

It wasn't fair the way her smirking mouth heated his blood and sent his thoughts everywhere but battle. If she felt a similar distraction when she faced him, she didn't show it. She was all deadly grace and beautiful boldness, now that her true identity had been revealed.

Theseus drew a deep breath and told himself to focus. He adjusted his grip on his sword, forced his muscles to ease, and faced Hippolyta. "More than ready."

He didn't yell or give any other signal. He simply lunged, swinging his sword and testing her reactions.

She parried without so much as a start or a blink to show she had been surprised.

He stepped in closer, trying to put his taller height and heavier frame to good use. He hammered his sword down at her.

She swayed back, flicking her sword to parry his weapon to the side, using his own momentum to send the tip of his sword into the sand.

Theseus stumbled, then threw himself to the side as she darted her sword toward his chest. A line of pain sliced along the top of his shoulder, and he nearly dropped his sword.

"Is that the best you can do?" She lightly hopped

back a step, giving him room to collect himself instead of pressing her advantage.

Though, she didn't have to press. She had clearly shown she could have ended him right then and there had she wanted. Giving him space was a power play, not mercy.

Theseus gathered himself, righted his stance, and forced his mind to calm. He had to do better than this if he had any hope of winning her hand.

Hippolyta waited, her stance balanced and light.

Theseus gritted his teeth. She was forcing him to take the offensive.

He swung low, aiming for her knees. She hopped over his swing, thrusting at his stomach.

As he dodged to the side, he turned his backswing to go high. She parried before twisting her move into another slice, this one burning pain along his ribs.

He sucked in a breath and went on the attack, trading blow after blow with her. As hard as he tried, all he managed to do was give her a slight scratch along the back of one wrist.

She didn't slacken, her reflexes never faltering. Her light blue eyes glowed with a fierce light. Her face shone with her grin, as if this combat filled her with joy.

That joy was mesmerizing. If Theseus could, he would step back and simply watch her in this deadly dance.

She dropped, sweeping out a foot. Next thing he knew, he was flat on his back, staring up at blue sky and her golden hair.

Kicking his sword out of his hand, she pressed the tip

of her own sword to his throat. "You have lost, King Theseus."

His heart throbbed in his throat, his chest twisting.

He'd lost. All this time, all this effort, and yet, in the end, he had failed.

The joyful sparkle to Hippolyta's eyes hardened into a cold glint more reminiscent of the swordmaiden who had been playing her role during his trials. She stepped back, lowering her sword. "You have failed to win my hand. It is time for you to leave."

What was going on? That was it?

"Hippolyta, wait." Theseus rolled to his feet. Surely she wasn't just going to toss him off the island. He'd felt a spark between them. Hadn't she felt it too?

Yet she spun on her heel, placing her back to him. "Throw him off our island."

"Hippolyta…" He didn't understand. After all the time they had spent together, it couldn't just end like this. Could it? "Will you at least send swordmaidens to save my Court? Please. It's all I ask."

She kept marching away from him, giving no indication that she even heard him.

The real Ariadne and another swordmaiden stepped into the arena. They gripped Theseus's arms and dragged him backwards. Another swordmaiden picked up Theseus's sword and followed them, cutting off his view of Hippolyta.

Apparently, she had not felt the same things he had. For some reason, that hurt even more than failing his Court.

THESEUS SLUMPED against the windowsill in his study, staring down at the evening light glinting off the Library's dome.

One week until Midsummer Night. Still no word from Hippolyta. Perhaps she really had washed her hands of him and his Court. If that was the case, then she was not the person he'd thought she was.

Then again, she had deceived him into thinking she was a handmaiden named Ariadne for most of their acquaintance. She literally wasn't the person he thought she was for most of the time he'd known her.

"Your Majesty?" Philostrate's voice came from behind him. "Are you all right, sire?"

Theseus released a long breath and pushed away from the window to face his steward. "I'm fine."

Philostrate's gaze searched his, then he shook his head. "You haven't been yourself ever since you returned from the Court of Swordmaidens."

Theseus wasn't going to tell Philostrate about Hippolyta and the constant ache in his heart ever since. He focused on the floor rather than on his steward. "I failed, and now the Court will likely be overrun on Midsummer Night."

"There is always the Court of Sand or Stone or any of the other Courts we can turn to. We aren't out of options." Philostrate's tone remained neutral.

"Perhaps. But the cost to bargain with another Court will be high. Perhaps higher than we are willing to pay." Theseus itched to slump against the windowsill yet again.

He had paid for this attempt to save his Court with his heart. Maybe another bargain wouldn't be so dreadful.

Yet he couldn't bring himself to give up on Hippolyta. Surely she would come. She would save his Court.

Even if she didn't love him the way he had come to love her.

Chapter Eight

Something cold and sharp jabbed his chest. Theseus started awake, blinking at the glow from the faerie lights bobbing near the ceiling now that someone had called them into brightening.

Dressed in her full battle regalia, complete with a chainmail tunic and a golden crown tucked into her hair, Queen Hippolyta stood next to his bed, her sword drawn and menacing him. Ariadne, her black hair in a braid, flanked Hippolyta, guarding her back.

Theseus wasn't sure if he should reach for a weapon or dredge up the last of his charm and pretend he was nonchalant about this queen showing up in his bedroom.

As he didn't have any other choices, he went with the second option. He placed one hand behind his head as if he were relaxed. "Queen Hippolyta. This is a surprise. It seems you could not resist my charms after all."

She smirked and tapped his bare chest with the flat of her sword. "King Theseus, I have conquered you and your Court. You have no choice but to yield to me."

What was going on? What was she doing here? Sending a few of her swordmaidens to help out on Midsummer Night was one thing, but this was not what he had expected.

His blood ran cold. All those times she'd asked him about his Court and his castle, had it all been another trick? Had she been setting him up so that she could conquer his Court without a battle?

She had betrayed him. Used his friendship to take over his Court.

He met her gaze, opening his mouth to spew anger at her.

Yet instead of the hardness he had been expecting, her eyes were soft. Almost begging something from him.

Whatever gentleness in her eyes, her voice remained hard as she rested the flat of her sword against his skin. "Yield, King Theseus."

What was she trying to tell him?

Either he remained angry, or he trusted her one more time. Hippolyta never did anything without a good reason. She had shown him that over and over again. Perhaps she was nothing but a cold, calculating woman who had planned all along to steal his Court from under him.

Or this was actually for the benefit of both their Courts.

It was time to trust her. One last time.

He trailed a finger up the flat of her sword. "I yield, Hippolyta. You have conquered me."

Her pink lips twitched, as if she wanted to smirk but wasn't ready to drop the hard façade just yet. "Then I have one last test for you. I ask you again, what benefit will you provide to my Court?"

For all of Hippolyta's tests, this question was the most important. He'd answered wrong the first time. He couldn't afford to give the wrong answer a second time.

His mind raced, as he thought back through his experiences in the Court of Swordmaidens. The pain in Hippolyta's voice when she talked about leaving her family in the Court of Sand. The way no married women were allowed to remain on the island with their husbands and families.

And he knew what answer he needed to give. He met and held Hippolyta's gaze. "My Court can provide a refuge when your Court can't. My Court can be a place where married women can still serve as swordmaidens, even though they can no longer live on your island. They can stay here with their families. My Court can make yours whole."

Her smile spread across her face. Not her smirk nor her battle grin. This was a genuine, joyful smile. She lifted her sword and rested its tip on the floor instead of his chest. "That would only work if our Courts were united in a true alliance that only a marriage between rulers can forge."

"But I thought that if I won your hand, that you would have to give up your crown." Theseus pushed onto an elbow, studying her. That was the cost she must pay if he had won her hand through the trials. He saw that now.

"True. But if I win your hand, that's a different story." Hippolyta's smile took on a teasing tilt. "If a swordmaiden's hand is won from her, she is forced to leave. But if I, instead, win your hand, I keep my crown."

Theseus flopped back onto his pillow and laughed. With all her tricks and schemes, she had been playing the long game to make sure they both got what they wanted. That was why she had trounced him in their duel and had him tossed off the island. There had been no other way.

More than that, having swordmaidens permanently stationed here would protect the Court of Knowledge not just on Midsummer Night, but for a long time to come. This victory was not just for one night, but for as long as he and Hippolyta lived.

He held out his hand. "You have already stolen my heart. You might as well claim my hand too."

She sheathed her sword, then clasped his hand. As their fingers met, a glow surrounded their hands. A binding, tying them together in the way of their peoples. They would need to be bound in marriage to complete the binding in full, but this was its start.

Theseus let Hippolyta tug him to his feet. He was barefoot, his trousers rumpled from sleep. He was not at his most kingly right now.

But that didn't matter as he cradled Hippolyta's face and kissed her as he'd longed to do.

After a long moment, Ariadne gave a cough. "Your Majesty, perhaps we should tell the swordmaidens to stand down? I'm sure the king's Court is growing restless, thinking they have been attacked."

Reluctantly, Theseus pulled away, still keeping an arm around Hippolyta's waist. "I suppose we should reassure my Court that everything is all right. I am eager to introduce them to the warrior who will soon be their queen."

Hippolyta grinned at him, then leaned in for another quick kiss, murmuring, "You may not have won my hand, but it seems your charms stole my heart after all."

They would have plenty of details to work out, like how to make their marriage work when he wasn't allowed to visit her Court. They still had to face Midsummer Night with all its dangerous monsters.

But with this queen at his side, Theseus would be able to take on anything. No monster would be as fierce, as deadly, as this queen of the swordmaidens.

STOLEN MIDSUMMER BRIDE

Steal a bride. Save the library. Try not to die.

Basil, a rather scholarly fae, works as an assistant librarian at the Great Library of the Court of Knowledge. Lonely and unwilling to join the yearly Midsummer Revel to find a mate, Basil takes the advice of his talking horse companion and decides to steal a human bride instead.

But Basil never expected to find a human girl waiting for him, wanting to be snatched. Nor had he expected a girl like Meg, an illiterate farmgirl who has no use for books.

With the barrier with the Realm of Monsters wearing thin and the chaos of Midsummer Night about to descend, will this unlikely pair put aside their differences long enough to save the Great Library from destruction? And maybe find a spark of love along the way?

From Tara Grayce, the author of the bestselling ELVEN ALLIANCE series, comes a new fae romantic fantasy inspired by Shakespeare's A Midsummer Night's Dream.

Read on Kindle Today!

Night of Secrets

A VILLAIN'S EVER AFTER

Bluebeard and the Outlaw

PRINCESS BY NIGHT

Lost in Averell

Acknowledgments

Thanks so much for reading *Steal a Swordmaiden's Heart*! While this book is short, it is one of my favorites. Theseus and Hippolyta have some of my best banter between romantic leads.

Thank you to my dad, mom, brothers, and sisters-in-law for always being so amazing! Thanks to Molly, Morgan, Addy, Sierra, and all my writer friends who have encouraged me through all the ups and downs of this writing journey. A special thank you to my proofreaders Mindy and Deborah who help clean up these books from my typos. Any mistakes that remain are purely my own.

www.ingramcontent.com/pod-product-compliance
Lightning Source LLC
Chambersburg PA
CBHW070316190726
48291CB00013B/1715